BRIDE OF THE DARK ONE

BRIDE OF THE DARK ONE

by Florence Verbell Brown

The outcasts; the hunted of all the brighter worlds, crowded onto Yaroto. But even here was there salvation for Ransome, the jinx-scarred acolyte, when tonight was the night of Bani-tai . . . the night of expiation by the photo-memoried priests of dark Darion?

The last light in the Galaxy was a torch. High in the rafters of Mytor's Cafe Yaroto it burned, and its red glare illuminated a gallery of the damned. Hands that were never far from blaster or knife; eyes that picked a hundred private hells out of the swirling smoke where a woman danced.

She was good to look at, moving in time to the savage rhythm of the music. The single garment she wore bared her supple body, and thighs and breasts and a cloud of dark hair wove a pattern of desire in the close room.

Fat Mytor watched, and his little crafty eyes gleamed. The Earth-girl danced like a she-devil tonight. The tables were crowded with the outcast and the hunted of all the brighter worlds. The woman's warm body, moving in the torchlight, would stir memories that men had thought they left light years behind. Gold coins would shower into Mytor's palm for bad wine, for stupor and forgetfulness.

Mytor sipped his imported amber kali, and the black eyes moved with seeming casualness, penetrating the deep shadows where the tables were, resting briefly on each drunken, greedy or fear-ridden face.

It was an old process with Mytor, nearly automatic. A glance told him enough, the state of a man's mind and senses and wallet. This trembling wreck, staring at the woman and nursing a glass of the cheapest green Yarotian wine, had spent his last silver. Mytor would have him thrown out. Another, head down and muttering over a tumbler of raw whiskey, would pass out before the night was over, and wake in an alley blocks away, with his gold in Mytor's pocket. A third wanted a woman, and Mytor knew what kind of a woman.

When the dance was nearly over Mytor heaved out of his chair, drew the rich folds of his native Venusian tarab about his bulk, and padded softly to a corner of the room, where the shadows lay deepest. Smiling, he rested a moist, jeweled paw on the table at which Ransome, the Earthman, sat alone.

Blue eyes looked up coldly out of a weary, lean face. The voice was bored.

"I've paid for my bottle and I have nothing left for you to steal. We have nothing in common, no business together. Now, if you don't mind, you're in my line of vision, and I'd like to watch the finish of the dance."

The fat Venusian's smile only broadened.

"May I sit down, Mr. Ransome?" he persisted. "Here, out of your line of vision?"

"The chair belongs to you," Ransome observed flatly.

"Thank you."

Covertly, as he had done for hours now, Mytor studied the gaunt, pale Earthman in the worn space harness. Ransome had apparently dismissed the Venusian renegade already, and his cold blue eyes followed the woman's every movement with fixed intensity.

The music swept on toward its climax and the woman's body was a storm of golden flesh and tossing black hair. Mytor saw the Earthman's pale lips twist in the faint suggestion of a bitter smile, saw the long fingers tighten around the glass.

Every man had his price on Yaroto, and Ransome would not be the first Mytor had bought with a woman. For a moment, Mytor watched the desire brighten in Ransome's eyes, studied the smile that some men wear on the way to death, in the last moment when life is most precious.

*

In this moment Ransome was for sale. And Mytor had a proposition.

"You were not surprised that I knew your name, Mr. Ransome?"

"Let's say that I wasn't interested."

Mytor flushed but Ransome was looking past him at the woman. The Venusian wiped his forehead with a soiled handkerchief, drummed fat fingers on the table for a moment, tried a different tack.

"Her name is Irene. She's lovely, isn't she, Mr. Ransome? Surely the inner worlds showed you nothing like her. The eyes, the red mouth, the breasts like—"

"Shut up," Ransome grated, and the glass shattered between his clenched fingers.

"Very well, Mr. Ransome." Whiskey trickled from the edge of the table in slow, thick drops, staining Mytor's white tarab. Ice was in the Venusian's voice. "Get out of my place—now. Leave the whiskey, and the woman. I have no traffic with fools."

Ransome sighed.

"I've told you, Mytor that you're wasting your time. But make your pitch, if you must."

"Ah, Mr. Ransome, you do not care to go out into the starless night. Perhaps there are those who wait for you, eh? With very long knives?"

Reflex brought Ransome's hand up in a lightning arc to the blaster bolstered under his arm, but Mytor's damp hand was on his wrist, and Mytor's purr was in his ear, the words coming quickly.

"You would die where you sit, you fool. You would not live even to know the sharpness of the long knives, the sacred knives of Darion, with the incantations inscribed upon their blades against blasphemers of the Temple."

Ransome shuddered and was silent. He saw Mytor's guards, vigilant in the shadows, and his hand fell away from the blaster.

When the dance was ended, and the blood was running hot and strong in him, he turned to face Mytor. His voice was impatient now, but his meaning was shrouded in irony.

"Are you trying to sell me a lucky charm, Mytor?"

The Venusian laughed.

"Would you call a space ship a lucky charm, Mr. Ransome?"

"No," Ransome said grimly. "If it were berthed across the street I'd be dead before I got halfway to it."

"Not if I provided you with a guard of my men."

"Maybe not. But I wouldn't have picked you for a philanthropist, Mytor."

"There are no philanthropists on Yaroto, Mr. Ransome. I offer you escape, it is true; you will have guessed that I expect some service in return."

"Get to the point." Ransome's eyes were weary now that the woman's dancing no longer held them. And there was little hope in his voice.

A man can put off a date across ten years, and across a hundred worlds, and there can be whiskey and women to dance for him. But there was a ship with burned-out jets lying in the desert outside this crumbling city, and it was the night of Bani-tai, the night of expiation in distant Darion, and Ransome knew that for him, this was the last world.

After tonight the priests would proclaim the start of a new Cycle, and the old debts, if still unpaid, would be canceled forever.

Ransome shrugged, a hopeless gesture. Enough of the cult of the Dark One lingered in the very stuff of his nerves and brain to tell him that the will of the Temple would be done.

But Mytor was speaking again, and Ransome listened in spite of himself.

"All the scum of the Galaxy wash up on Yaroto at last," the fat Venusian said. "That is why you and I are here, Mr. Ransome. It is also why a certain pirate landed his ship on the desert out there three days ago. *Callisto Queen*, the ship's name is, though it has borne a dozen others. Cargo—Jovian silks and dyestuffs from the moons of Mars, narco-vin from the system of Alpha Centauri."

Mytor paused, put the tips of fat fingers together, and looked hard at Ransome.

"Is all of that supposed to mean something to me?" Ransome asked. A waiter had brought over a glass to replace the broken one, and he poured a drink for himself, not inviting Mytor. "It doesn't."

"It suggests a course, nothing more. In toward Sol, out to Yaroto by way of Alpha Centauri. Do you follow the courses of pirate ships, Mr. Ransome?"

"One," Ransome said savagely. "I've lost track of her."

"Perhaps you know the *Callisto Queen* better under her former name, then."

Again Ransome's hand moved toward the blaster, and this time Mytor made no attempt to stop him. Ransome's thin lips tightened with some powerful emotion, and he half rose to look hard at Mytor.

"The name of the ship?"

"Her captain used to call her *Hawk of Darion.*"

Ransome understood. *Hawk of Darion,* hell ship driving through black space under the command of a man he had once sworn to kill. Eight years rolled back and he saw them together, laughing at him: the Earthman-captain and the woman who had been Ransome's.

"Captain Jareth," Ransome said slowly. "Here—on Yaroto."

The Venusian nodded, pushing the bottle toward Ransome. The Earthman ignored the gesture.

"Is the woman with him?"

Mytor smiled his feline smile. "You would like to see her blood run under the knives of the priests, no?"

"No."

Ransome meant it. Somewhere, in the years of flight, he had lost his love for the blonde, red-lipped Dura-ki, and with it had gone his bitter hatred and his desire for revenge.

He jerked his mind back to the present, to Mytor.

"And if I told you that it must be her life or yours?" Mytor was asking him.

Ransome's eyes widened. He sensed that Mytor's last question was not, an idle one. He leaned forward and asked:

"How do you fit into this at all, Mytor?"

"Easily. Once, ten years ago, you and the woman now aboard the *Hawk of Darion* blasphemed together against the Temple of the Dark One, in Darion."

"Go on," Ransome said.

"When you landed here this afternoon the avenging priests were not far behind you."

"How did you—"

"I have many contacts," Mytor purred. "I find them invaluable. But you are growing impatient, Mr. Ransome. I will be brief. I have contracted with the priests of Darion to deliver you to them tonight for a considerable sum."

"How did you know you would find me?"

"I was given your description." He made a gesture that took in all the occupants of the torch-lit room. "So many of the hunted, and the haunted, come here to forget for an hour the things that pursue them. I was expecting you, Mr. Ransome."

"If there is a large sum of money involved, I'm sure you'll make every effort to carry out your part of the bargain," Ransome observed ironically.

"I am a businessman, it is true. But in my dealings with the master of the *Hawk of Darion* I have seen the woman and I have heard stories. It occurred to me that the priests would pay much more for the woman than they would for you, and it seemed to me that a message from you might coax her off the ship. After all, when one has been in love—"

"That's enough." Ransome had risen to his feet. "I wonder if I could kill you before your guards got to me."

"Are you then so in love with death, Ransome?" The Venusian spoke quickly. "Don't be a fool. It is a small thing, a woman's life—a woman who has betrayed you."

Ransome stood silent, his arm halfway to his blaster. The woman had begun to dance again in the red glare of the torch.

"There will be other women," the Venusian was murmuring. "The woman who dances now, I will give her to you, to take with you in your new ship."

Ransome looked slowly from the glowing body of the woman to the guards around the walls, down into Mytor's confident face. His arm dropped away from the blaster.

"Any man—for a price." The Venusian's murmur was lost in the blare of the music. Ransome had eased his lean body back into the chair.

*

The night air was cold against Ransome's cheek when he went out an hour later, surrounded by Mytor's men. Yaroto's greenish moon was overhead now, but its pale light did not help him to see more clearly. It only made shadows in every doorway and twisting alley.

Mytor's car was only a few feet away but before he could reach it he was shoved aside by one of the Venusian's guards. At the same moment the night flamed with the blue-yellow glare from a dozen blasters. Ransome raised his own weapon, staring into the shadows, seeking his attackers.

"That's our job. Get in," said one of the guards, wrenching open the car door.

Then the firing was over as suddenly as it had begun. The guards clustered at the opening of an alley down the street. Mytor's driver sat impassively in the front seat.

When the guards returned one of them thrust something at Ransome, something hard and cold. He glanced at it. A long knife.

There was no need to read the inscription on the hilt. He knew it by heart.

"Death to him who defileth the Bed of the Dark One. Life to the Temple and City of Darion."

Once Ransome would have pocketed the knife as a kind of grim keepsake. Now he only let it fall to the floor.

In the brief, ghostly duel just over he had neither seen nor heard his attackers. That added, somehow, to the horror of the thing.

He shrugged off the thought, turning his mind to the details of the plan by which he would save his life.

It was quite simple. Ransome had been in space long enough to know where the crewmen went on a strange world. Half an hour later he sat with a gunner from the *Hawk of Darion*, in one of the gaudy pleasure houses clustered on the fringe of the city near the spaceport and the desert beyond.

"Will you take the note to the Captain's woman?"

The man squirmed, avoiding Ransome's ice-blue stare.

"Captain killed the last man who looked at his woman," the gunner muttered sullenly. "Flogged him to death."

"I'm not asking you to look at her," Ransome reminded him.

The gunner sat looking at the stack of Mytor's money piled on the table before him. A woman drifted over.

"Go away," Ransome said, without raising his eyes. He added another bill to the stack.

"Let me see the note before I take it," the gunner demanded.

"It would mean nothing to you." Ransome pushed a half-empty bottle toward the man, poured him out another drink.

The man's hands were trembling with inner conflict as he measured the killing lash against the stack of yellow Yarotian kiroons, and the pleasures it would buy him. He drank, dribbling a little of the wine down his grimy chin, and then returned to the subject of seeing the note, with drunken persistence.

"I got to see it first."

"It's in a language you wouldn't—"

"Let him see it," a new voice cut in. "Translate it for him, Mr. Ransome."

*

It was a woman's voice, cold and contemptuous. Ransome looked up quickly, and at first he didn't recognize her. The gunner never took his eyes from the stack of kiroons on the table.

"Let him see how a man murders a woman to save his own neck."

"You're supposed to be dancing at Mytor's place," Ransome said. "That's your business; this is mine."

He closed his hand over the gunner's wrist as the man reached convulsively for the money, menaced now by the angry woman.

"Half now, the rest later." Ransome's eyes burned into the crewman's. The latter looked away. Ransome tightened his grip, and pain contorted the gunner's features.

"Look at me," Ransome said. "If you cross me you'll wish you could die by flogging."

The woman Mytor had called Irene was still standing by the table when the gunner had left with the note and his money.

"Aren't you going to ask me to sit down?"

"Certainly. Sit down."

"I'd like a drink."

She sipped her wine in silence and Ransome studied her by the flickering light of the candle burning on the table between them.

She wore a simple street dress now, in contrast to the gaudy, revealing garments of the pleasure house women. The beauty of her soft, unpainted lips, her golden skin and wide-set green eyes was more striking now, seen at close range, than it had been in the smoky cavern of Mytor's place.

"What are you thinking now, Ransome?"

The question was unexpected, and Ransome answered without forethought: "The Temple."

"You studied for the priesthood of the Dark One yourself."

"Did Mytor tell you that?"

Irene nodded. The candlelight gave luster to her dark hair and revealed the contours of her high, firm breasts.

Ransome's pulse speeded up just looking at her. Then he saw that she was regarding him as if he were something crawling in damp stone, and there was bitterness in him.

"There are things that even Mytor doesn't know, even omniscient Mytor—"

He checked himself.

"Well?"

"Nothing."

"You were going to tell me about how you are really a very honorable man. Why don't you? You have an hour before it will be time to betray the woman from the *Hawk of Darion*."

Ransome shrugged, and his voice returned her mockery.

"If I told you that I had been an acolyte in the Temple of the Dark One, and that I was condemned to death for blasphemy, committed for love of a woman, would you like me better?"

"I might."

13

"Ten years ago," Ransome said. He talked, and the mighty walls of the Temple reared themselves around his mind, and the music of the pleasure house became the chanting of the priests at the high altar.

*

He stood at the rear of the great Temple, and he had the tonsure and the black robes, and his name was not Ransome, but Ra-sed.

He had almost forgotten his Terran name. Forgotten, too, were his parents, and the laboratory ship that had been his home until the crash landing that had left him an orphan and Ward of the Temple.

Red candles burned before the high altar, but terror began just beyond their flickering light. It was dark where Ra-sed stood, and he could hear the cries of the people in the courtyard outside, and feel the trembling of the pillars, the very pillars of the Temple, and the groaning of stone on massive stone in the great, shadowed arches overhead. Above all, the chanting before the altar of the Dark One, rising, rising toward hysteria.

And then, like a knife in the darkness, the scream, and the straining to see which of the maidens the sacred lots cast before the altar had chosen; and the sudden, sick knowledge that it was Dura-ki. Dura-ki, of the soft golden hair and bright lips.

In stunned silence, Ra-sed, acolyte, listened to the bridal chant of the priests; the ancient words of the Dedication to the Dark One.

The chant told of the forty times forty flights of onyx steps leading downward behind the great altar to the dwelling place of the Dark One and of the forty terrible beasts couched in the pit to guard His slumber.

In the beginning, Dalir, the Sire, God of the Mists, had gone down wrapped in a sea fog, and had stolen the Sacred Fire while the Dark One slept. All life in Darion had come from Dalir's mystic union with the Sacred Fire.

Centuries passed before a winter of bitter frosts came, and the Dark One awakened cold in His dwelling place and found the Sacred Fire stolen. His wrath moved beneath the city then, and Darion crashed in shattered ruin and death.

Those who were left had hurled a maiden screaming into the greatest of the clefts in the earth, that the bed of the Idol might be warmed by an ember of the stolen Fire. Later, they had raised His awful Temple on the spot.

So it had been, almost from the beginning. When the pillars of the Temple shook, a maiden was chosen by the Sacred Lots to go down as a bride to the Dark One, lest He destroy the city and the people.

The chant had come to an end. The legend had been told once more.

They led her forth then—Dura-ki, the chosen one. Shod in golden sandals, and wearing the crimson robe of the ritual, she moved out of Ra-sed's sight, behind the high altar. No acolyte was permitted to approach that place.

The chanting was a thing of wild delirium now, and Ra-set placed a cold hand to steady himself against a trembling pillar. He heard the drawing of the ancient bolts, the booming echo as the great stone was drawn aside, and he closed his eyes, as though that could shut out the vision of the monstrous pit.

But his ears he could not close, and he heard the scream of Dura-ki, his own betrothed, as they threw her to the Idol.

*

At the table in the Yarotian pleasure house, Ransome's thin lips were pale. He swallowed his drink.

The woman opposite him was nearly forgotten now, and when he went on, it was for himself, to rid himself of things that had haunted him down all the bleak worlds to his final night of betrayal and death. His eyes were empty, fixed on another life. He did not see the change that crossed Irene's face, did not see the cold contempt fade away, to be replaced slowly with understanding. She leaned forward, lips slightly parted, to hear the end of his story.

For the love of golden-haired Dura-ki, the acolyte, Ra-sed, had gone down into the pit of the Dark one, where no mortal had gone before, except as a sacrifice.

He had hidden himself in the gloom of the pillars when the others left in chanting procession after the ceremony. Now he was wrenching at the rusted bolts that held the stone in place. It seemed to him that the rumbling grew in the earth beneath his feet and in the blackness of the vaulting overhead. Terror was in him, for his blasphemy would bring death to Darion. But the vision of Dura-ki was in him too, giving strength to tortured muscles. The bolts came away with a metallic screech, piercing against the mutter of shifting stone.

He was turning to the heavy ring set in the stone when he caught a glimmer of reflected light in an idol's eye. Swiftly he crouched behind the great stone, waiting.

The priests came, two of them, bearing torches. Knives flashed as Ra-sed sprang, but he wrenched the blade from the hand of the first, buried it in the throat of the second. The man fell with a cry, but a stunning blow from behind sent Ra-sed sprawling across the fallen body. The other priest was on him, choking out his life.

The last torch fell; and Ra-sed twisted savagely, lashed out blindly with the long knife. There was a sound of rending cloth, a muttered curse in the darkness, and the fingers ground harder into Ra-sed's throat. Black tides washed over his mind, and he never remembered the second and last convulsive thrust of the knife that let out the life of the priest.

He did remember straining against the ring of the great stone. The echo boomed out for the second time that night, as the stone moved away at last, to lay bare the realm of the Dark One.

Bitterness touched Ransome's eyes as he spoke now, the bitterness of a man who has lost his God.

"There were no onyx steps, no monsters waiting beneath the stone. The legends were false."

Ransome turned his glass slowly, staring into its amber depths. Then he became aware of Irene, waiting for him to go on.

"I got her out," Ransome said shortly. "I went down into that stinking pit and I got Dura-ki out. The air was nearly unbreathable where I found her.

She was unconscious on a ledge at the end of a long slope. Hell itself might have been in the pit that opened beneath it. A geologist would have called it a major fault, but it was hell enough. When I picked her up, I found the bones of all those others . . . ."

Irene's green eyes had lost their coldness. She let her hand rest on his for a moment. But her voice was puzzled.

"This Dura-ki—she is the woman on the *Hawk of Darion?*"

Ransome nodded. He stood up. His lips were a hard, thin line.

"My little story has an epilogue. Something not quite so romantic. I lived with Dura-ki in hiding near Darion for a year, until a ship came in from space. A pirate ship, with a tall, good-looking Earthman for a master. I took passage for Dura-ki, and signed on myself as a crewman. A fresh start in a bright, new world." Ransome laughed shortly. "I'll spare you the details of that happy voyage. At the first port of call, on Jupiter, Dura-ki stood at the top of the gangway and laughed when her Captain Jareth had me thrown off the ship."

"She betrayed you for the master of the *Hawk of Darion*," Irene said softly.

"And tonight she'll pay," Ransome finished coldly. He threw down a few coins to pay for their drinks. "It's been pleasant telling you my pretty little story."

"Ransome, wait. I—"

"Forget it," Ransome said.

*

Mytor's car was waiting, and Ransome could sense the presence of the guards lurking in the dark, empty street.

"The spaceport," Ransome told his driver. "Fast."

He thought of the note he had given the crewman to deliver:

"Ra-sed would see his beloved a last time before he dies."

"Faster," Ransome grated, and the powerful car leapt forward into the night.

*

Ships, like the men who drove them, came to Yaroto to die. Three quarters of the spaceport was a vast jungle of looming black shapes, most of them awaiting the breaker's hammer. Ransome dismissed the car and threaded his way through the deserted yards with the certainty of a man used to the ugly places of a hundred worlds.

Mytor had suggested the meeting place, a hulk larger than most, a cruiser once in the fleet of some forgotten power.

Ransome had fought in the ships of half a dozen worlds. Now the ancient cruiser claimed his attention. Martian, by the cut of her rusted braking fins. Ransome tensed, remembering the charge of the Martian cruisers in the Battle of Phoebus. Since then he had called himself an Earthman, because, even if his parentage had not given him claim to that title already, a man who had been in the Earth ships at Phoebus had a right to it.

He was running a hand over the battered plate of a blast tube when Dura-ki found him. She was a smaller shadow moving among the vast, dark hulls. With a curious, dead feeling in him, Ransome stepped away from the side of the cruiser to meet her.

"Ra-sed, I could not let you die alone—"

Because her voice was a ghost from the past, because it stirred things in him that had no right to live after all the long years that had passed, Ransome acted before Dura-ki could finish speaking. He hit her once, hard; caught the crumpling body in his arms, and started back toward Mytor's car. If he remembered another journey in the blackness with this woman in his arms, he drove the memory back with the savage blasphemies of a hundred worlds.

*

On the rough floor of Mytor's place, Dura-ki stirred and groaned.

Ransome didn't like the way things were going. He hadn't planned to return to the Cafe Yaroto, to wait with Mytor for the arrival of the priests.

"There are a couple of my men outside," Mytor told him. "When the priests are spotted you can slip out through the rear exit."

"Why the devil do I have to be here now?"

"As I have told you, I am a businessman. Until I have turned the girl over to the priests I cannot be sure of my payment. This girl, as you know, is not without friends. If Captain Jareth knew that she was here he would tear this place apart, he and his crew. Those men have rather an impressive reputation as fighters, and while my guard here—"

"You've been drinking too much of your own rotten liquor, Mytor. Why should I try to save her at the eleventh hour? To hand her back to her lover?"

"I never drink my own liquor, Mr. Ransome." He took a sip of his kali in confirmation. "I have seen love take many curious shapes."

Ransome stood up. "Save your memoirs. I want a guard to get me to the ship you promised me. And I want it now."

Mytor did not move. The guards, ranged around the walls, stood silent but alert.

"Mytor."

"Yes, Mr. Ransome?"

"There isn't any ship. There never was."

The Venusian shrugged. "It would have been easier for you if you hadn't guessed. I'm really sorry."

"So you'll make a double profit on this deal. I was the bait for Dura-ki, and Irene was bait for me. You are a good businessman, Mytor."

"You are taking this rather better than I had expected, Mr. Ransome."

Ransome slumped down into his chair again. He felt no fear, no emotion at all. Somewhere, deep inside, he had known from the beginning that there would be no more running away after tonight, that the priests would have their will with him. Perhaps he had been too tired to care. And there had been Irene, planted by Mytor to fill his eyes, to make him careless and distracted.

He wondered if Irene had known of her role, or had been an unconscious tool, like himself. With faint surprise, he found himself hoping that she had not acted against him intentionally.

*

Dura-ki was unconscious when the priests came. She had looked at Ransome only once, and he had stared down at his hands.

Now she stood quietly between two of the black-robed figures, watching as others counted out gold coins into Mytor's grasping palm. Her eyes betrayed neither hope nor fear, and she did not shrink from the burning, fanatical stares of the priests, nor from their long knives. The pirate's consort was not the girl who had screamed in the dimness of the Temple when the Sacred Lots were cast.

A priest touched Ransome's shoulder and he started in spite of himself. He tried to steady himself against the sudden chill that seized him.

And then Dura-ki, who had called him once to blasphemy, now called him to something else.

"Stand up, Ra-sed. It is the end. The game is played out and we lose at last. It will not be worse than the pit of the Dark One."

Ransome got to his feet and looked at her. He no longer loved this woman but her quiet courage stirred him.

With an incredibly swift lunge he was on the priest who stood nearest Dura-ki. The man reeled backward and struck his skull against the wall. It was a satisfying sound, and Ransome smiled tightly, a half-forgotten oath of Darion on his lips.

He grabbed the man by the throat, spun him around, and sent him crashing into another.

A knife slashed at him, and he broke the arm that held it, then sprang for the door while the world exploded in blaster fire.

Dura-ki moved toward him. He wrenched at the door, felt the cold night air rash in. A hand clawed at the girl's shoulder, but Ransome freed her with a hard, well-aimed blow.

When she was outside, Ransome fought to give her time to get back to the *Hawk of Darion*. Also, he fought for the sheer joy of it. The air in his lungs was fresh again, and the taste of treachery was out of his mouth.

It took all of Mytor's guards and the priests to overpower him, but they were too late to save Mytor from the knife that left him gasping out his life on the floor.

Ransome did not struggle in the grip of the guards. He stood quietly, waiting.

"Your death will not be made prettier by what you have done," a priest told him. The knife was poised.

"That depends on how you look at it," Ransome answered.

"Does it?"

"Absolutely," a hard, dry voice answered from the doorway.

Ransome turned his head and had a glimpse of Irene. With her, a blaster level in his hand, and his crew at his back, was Captain Jareth. It was he who had answered the priest's last question.

Mytor had said that Jareth's crew had an impressive reputation as fighters, and he lived just long enough to see the truth of his words. The priests and the guards went down before the furious attack of the men from the *Hawk of Darion*. Ransome fought as one of them.

When it was over, it was not to Captain Jareth that he spoke, but to Irene.

"Why did you do this? You didn't know Dura-ki, and you despised me."

"At first I did. That's why I agreed to Mytor's plan. But when I had spoken to you, I felt differently. I—"

Jareth came over then, holstering his blaster. Irene fell silent.

The big spaceman shifted uneasily, then spoke to Ransome.

"I found Dura-ki near here. She told me what you did."

Ransome shrugged.

"I sent her back to the ship with a couple of my men."

Abruptly, Jareth turned and stooped over the still form of Mytor. From the folds of the Venusian's stained tarab he drew a ring of keys. He tossed them to Ransome.

"This will be the first promise that Mytor ever kept."

"What do you mean?"

"Those are the keys to his private ship. I'll see that you get to it."

It was Irene who spoke then. "That wasn't all that Mytor promised him." The two men looked at her in surprise. Then Ransome understood.

"Will you come with me, Irene?" he asked her.

"Where?" Her eyes were shining, and she looked very young.

Ransome smiled at her. "The Galaxy is full of worlds. And even the Dark One cancels his debts when the night of Bani-tai is over."

"Let's go and look at some of those worlds," Irene said.